THIS ANNUAL BELONGS TO

....

....

EGMONT
We bring stories to life

First published in Great Britain 2012
by Egmont UK Limited,
239 Kensington High Street, London W8 6SA

Text by Lizzie Catford. Design by Martin Aggett.
© 2012 Prism Art & Design Limited, a HIT Entertainment company.
Based on an original idea by D. Gingell, D. Jones and original
characters created by R. J. M. Lee.

ISBN 978 1 4052 6337 5
51511/3
Printed in Italy

Adult supervision is recommended when glue, paint, scissors
and other sharp points are in use.

HiT entertainment

CONTENTS

THE PRIDE OF PONTYPANDY

The firefighting crew are the pride of Pontypandy! Meet Fireman Sam and the rest of the team.

Sam

Fireman Sam is a hero! He is brave and strong.

Penny

Penny is a brave firefighter too. She is always calm in a crisis.

Elvis

Elvis never hesitates to help. He wants to be a hero like Sam one day.

Station Officer Steele

Station Officer Steele is in charge of the Pontypandy Fire Station.

Radar

Radar is a trained sniffer dog.

THE NEIGHBOURS OF PONTYPANDY

Meet the neighbours of Pontypandy, Fireman Sam's friends and family.

Dilys and Norman

Dilys works in the local shop. Naughty Norman is always causing mischief, but Dilys still thinks he's her little treasure!

Tom Thomas

Tom runs the Mountain Rescue Centre.

The Jones Family

Charlie Jones is Fireman Sam's brother. He is a fisherman. His wife Bronwyn runs the Wholefish Café. His children, Sarah and James, are twins!

The Flood Family

Helen Flood is a nurse. Whenever there is an accident, Nurse Helen rushes to help. Her husband Mike is the local handyman. Their daughter Mandy is a bit of a tomboy!

Trevor Evans

Trevor drives the Pontypandy bus.

OPEN DAY

It's Fire Station Open Day! The people of Pontypandy will be coming to see what the brave fire crew do.

Station Officer Steele runs through the plan with Sam, Penny and Elvis. There will be abseiling, a tour of Jupiter, a dog display and a rooftop rescue!

The children can't wait to see inside the Fire Station.

"I'm going up the ladder to put out a fire," boasts Naughty Norman Price.

"No you're not," laughs Mandy. "It's like a show. You'll watch Penny, Sam and Elvis."

Open Day begins. Penny abseils down from the Training Tower roof.

Naughty Norman wants a closer look. But Elvis sees and makes him stand behind the safety rope, like everyone else.

Aww, boring!

Nee Nah, Nee Nah! It's time for the tour of Jupiter.

Inside Jupiter's cab, Naughty Norman presses all the buttons. Luckily, Fireman Sam notices and turns them off again.

Jupiter isn't a toy, Norman.

Follow me!

Naughty Norman has a new idea ...

13

Norman and James go into the Fire Station garage.

"Should we be here?" asks James.

"Of course," says Norman. "It's Open Day!"

Norman pulls the lever to Venus' turntable.

Put it back, Norman.

Outside, Elvis is doing a dog display with Radar.

Elvis has an old black boot. He has hidden the other boot and Radar must find it.

Radar sniffs the boot and sets off.

Brilliant!

Go on, Radar!

WOOF WOOF

Good boy, Radar.

Radar finds the hidden boot in no time.

Did you hear that?

Inside the Fire Station, Norman is now sitting in Station Officer Steele's chair. He has his feet up on the desk!

He hears an announcement on the loudspeakers. *It's time for the rooftop rescue!*

Come on, James!

"Let's get the best seats in the house," Norman says to James.

He leads James up the fire escape onto the roof!

On the ground, the team get ready to perform the rescue.

Penny looks up and gasps when she recognises Norman and James on the roof!

15

On the roof, a sudden gust of wind makes James slip.

Now a real rooftop rescue is needed!

"This is a job for Jupiter," says Fireman Sam.

The team quickly get Jupiter's ladder out and Fireman Sam climbs up onto the roof.

He pulls James to safety.

Nearly there!

Fireman Sam gets Norman and James safely to the ground.

"You became the rooftop rescue," laughs Sam.

It's been a success, Sir!

Open Day is over. The team enjoy a nice cup of tea. Radar chews the boot he found earlier.

"That boot's a mess!" says Station Officer Steele.

Penny looks inside for a name ...

... Erm, it's one of yours, Sir!

JUPITER TO THE RESCUE!

Moving platform – so Fireman Sam can reach people who are in trouble.

In the story, Fireman Sam used Jupiter to rescue Norman Price and James Jones from the Fire Station roof. Jupiter is used in all kinds of emergencies, especially when there is a fire to put out.

Hose pipe connectors – so Fireman Sam can spray water to put out fires.

Flashing lights and a loud siren – so people clear the way when Jupiter rushes to an emergency.

18

GREAT FIRES OF PONTYPANDY!

There are lots of fires in Pontypandy! Guide Fireman Sam and Jupiter to all the fires so they can put them out, and then race to the finish.

START

FINISH

How many fires did Sam and Jupiter put out? Write the answer here:

Job done. What a team!

Answers on page 68.

SPOT THE DIFFERENCE

Look carefully at these pictures of the team. They look the same, but there are 5 differences. Can you spot them?

1

2

Answers on page 68.

CAT IN A FLAP!

Lion the cat is stuck on the roof! Trace the red line to see who Bronwyn calls for help. Then follow the yellow line to see who is sent to the rescue, and lastly the orange line to see who helps them.

Answers on page 68.

PIRATES OF PONTYPANDY

In Pontypandy the weather is nice and calm, but out at sea it's always important to be careful ...

Nice and calm today.

Fireman Sam and Charlie have been on a fishing trip.

How about a pirate's picnic?

When Sam and Charlie get out of the boat they see the children.

The children are playing pirates. But Norman and Sarah both want to be captain.

"Girls can't be captains," argues Norman.

"Yes, they can. Why not both be captains?" says Sam, fairly.

The children make a pirate's picnic and take it to the beach.

"Let's leave the girly pirates behind," Norman whispers to James. They sneak off!

They didn't even guard it!

Ooof. It's very heavy.

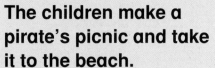

When Norman and James get hungry, they creep back and take the picnic hamper.

Ha, ha! They'll get a shock when they open the basket!

Sarah and Mandy are hiding behind a rock. They watch the boys take the picnic.

Naughty Norman makes James row them out to sea.

"It's what real pirates do," says Norman.

James and Norman are tired out.

"Let's have a pirate's nap," says Norman and they close their eyes.

When they wake up James opens the picnic basket. It's full of rocks!

"Never mind the picnic," says Norman. "Where are we?"

While they have been asleep the boat has drifted out to sea!

I'd better call Fireman Sam.

Meanwhile, Sarah and Mandy are worried.

They saw Norman and James go out in the boat, but they can't see them anywhere in the Harbour!

They go and tell Charlie.

Fireman Sam and Penny head out to sea in Neptune, to search for the boys.

Tom Thomas takes to the skies in Wallaby One, to try to spot Norman and James.

He soon sees them. He radios Fireman Sam to tell him where to find the boys.

Penny drives Neptune skilfully over the waves to reach the boys.

Fireman Sam pulls Norman and James to safety.

Fireman Sam gets the boys safely onto dry land.

"Do you think girls make good pirates now?" Sarah asks Norman.

"Umm," says Norman, remembering Penny steering Neptune over the waves ..."Yes, Captain Sarah, they do!"

SEA RESCUE!

Neptune is Pontypandy's very own lifeboat! Neptune is always on standby, ready to launch into the sea from the boathouse on Pontypandy Harbour.

Controls – so Penny can steer Neptune over the waves to reach anyone in trouble.

Bright yellow – so Neptune can still be spotted in stormy weather.

Light, waterproof material – so Neptune floats on water.

Penny is a trained coastguard, as well as a Fire Officer. She leads rescue missions out at sea.
◀◀◀ Colour in Penny.

OVERBOARD!

Norman has fallen overboard into the water! Penny and Elvis are rushing to rescue him in Neptune. Use your finger to zoom Neptune over the waves to Norman.

START

How many whales does Neptune pass?

FINISH

Answers on page 68.

NAUGHTY NORMAN

Fireman Sam has rescued Norman Price again!

"You must be more careful, laddie!" Station Officer Steele tells Norman.

What do you think Norman did this time?

Can you spot these close-ups in the big picture?

1
2
3
4

30

VENUS DOT-TO-DOT

Venus is a small rescue tender. The team use Venus when they need to get into places where big Jupiter can't fit!

Starting at number 1, join the dots to complete this picture of Venus, then colour it in.

ELVIS TO THE RESCUE

You can help read this story. Join in when you see a picture.

 Elvis
 Station Officer Steele
Mike
Norman

 has broken his leg.  takes on

firefighting duties, while  mans the

control desk. The first call comes in.  has

slipped while mending his TV aerial. Sam, Penny

and  rush to the rescue, leaving

 behind.

At the Floods' house,

is dangling from the roof. "I'll get

him down," says  .

But  muddles his orders and just gets

in the way.  radios the crew with

another emergency.  has his head stuck

in the railings! "I'll deal with it," says  .

"Sam and Penny, you can

finish off here."

"Please help my little boy," cries Dilys when

she sees  .  's head is stuck

tight. "Not to worry," says  . "I once

freed a little boy who had his head stuck like

this ... "  shows how the boy's head

was stuck, but now his head is stuck too!

Sam and Penny are still busy saving  ,

so  comes to the rescue himself!

 bends the railings to free

and  . Sam and Penny arrive. They've

rescued  . "All sorted here too,"

tells them. "Thanks to  , who is ready to

help, even with a broken leg!"

No need to share the details, eh!?

35

SPOTLIGHT ON ELVIS

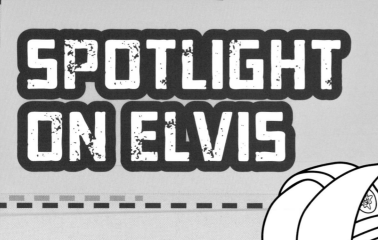

Elvis is proud to be a Fire Officer. When Elvis isn't fighting fires, he's practising his other passion, rock and roll!

Quick, it's an emergency! Colour in Elvis as he whizzes down the pole.

HERO TIME

Elvis wants to be brave and strong, just like Fireman Sam.

When two emergencies happen at the same time, Elvis must deal with one of them on his own. Follow the tangled lines to see who Fireman Sam helps and who Elvis helps.

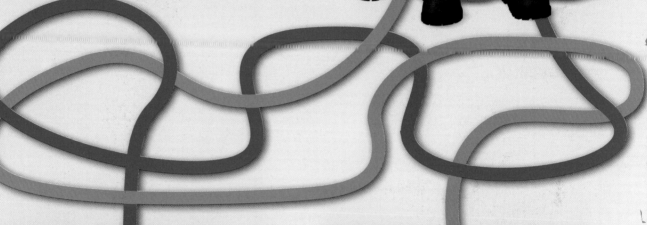

Trevor has set his barbecue on fire.

Answers on page 68.

Norman is stuck up a tree.

37

ODD ANIMAL OUT

These are some of the animals that live in Pontypandy. Can you spot the odd one out in each row?

Nipper

Lion

Woolly and Lambikins

Fox

Answers on page 68.

38

WHICH SAMS ARE THE SAME?

Look carefully at all these pictures of Fireman Sam. Can you spot two pictures that are exactly the same?

1

2

3

4

5

6

7

MANDY'S FLARE

Tom Thomas is looking after Nipper for the day. Nipper wants to play, but Tom has work to do.

Tom is checking the Mountain Rescue Kit.

Nipper brings him a stick. He wants to play fetch.

Tom throws the stick for Nipper.

Tom counts the Mountain Rescue flares.

"I, 2, 3, 4, 5," he counts.

Brrr Brrr, rings the phone. Tom goes to answer it.

Nipper comes back with his stick.

He sees the flares and thinks they're sticks as well!

He picks one up with his teeth and goes to find someone to play with.

40

Nipper trots over the hills, until he sees a large bird.

He drops the flare onto the ground and chases after the bird!

CAW CAW!

WOOF!

Go on!

No!

Meanwhile in Pontypandy, Naughty Norman is teasing Mandy. He wants her to do a skateboard jump, but Mandy doesn't want to.

Sorry, Mandy.

Mandy gets cross and goes home.

Norman follows her to say sorry.

"Come on, Mandy," says Norman. "Let's play hide-and-seek together instead."

41

Penny arrives at the Mountain Rescue Centre. She is going abseiling with Tom.

"I've got a problem," says Tom. "I've lost one of the flares."

Penny sets off without Tom. He stays behind to find the missing flare.

I counted 5. Now there are only 4.

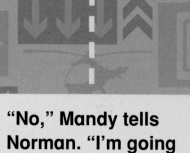

Whooosh! It'll be great!

It's not a toy.

The children are playing hide-and-seek, when they find the flare lying on the grass where Nipper left it.

"Let's set it off!" says Naughty Norman.

But Mandy isn't sure if that is a good idea. It could be dangerous!

Boring!

I don't care what you think.

"No," Mandy tells Norman. "I'm going to hand it in to Fireman Sam."

Uh-oh! HELP!

Up on the clifftop, Penny is abseiling. Suddenly the rope catches! Penny is stuck!

She tries to call for help, but she drops her mobile phone.

Oh, no!

Down on the ground, Norman and Mandy hear someone shouting for help.

They look up and see Penny.

"We'll get help," shouts Mandy.

43

Penny notices the flare.

"You shouldn't be playing with that!" she says.

"We were going to give it to Fireman Sam," says Norman, guiltily.

"Quite right," says Penny. "But right now it's just what I need."

Norman and Mandy throw Penny the flare. She sets it off.

whoosh

Tom sees the flare.

Someone's in trouble. I'd better call Fireman Sam.

Fireman Sam and Elvis rush to the rescue.

44

Tom flies Wallaby One, while Sam goes in the rescue harness. He reaches Penny and lifts her to safety.

Thank you.

"It's lucky you had that flare," Penny says to Norman and Mandy.

"Yes," says Fireman Sam. "Well done for not letting it off."

"Er, I always said it wasn't a toy," lies Naughty Norman.

That night Tom, Penny and Sam have a barbecue.

"It's a mystery how that flare disappeared," says Tom.

Just then Nipper grabs a string of sausages from the barbecue.

"Hmm, I think Nipper likes bangers!" laughs Sam.

MOUNTAIN RESCUE!

Tom Thomas leads mountain rescue missions. He uses his Rescue Jeep to reach people who are in trouble.

A roof rack for storing plenty of rescue equipment.

Tom wears a bright orange rescue outfit so he is easy to spot.

Big wheels keep the Jeep steady on uneven, mountain ground.

When he needs to reach a tough spot or get somewhere fast, Tom takes to the skies in Wallaby One, the Rescue Helicopter!

Quick, colour in Wallaby One before it flies away!

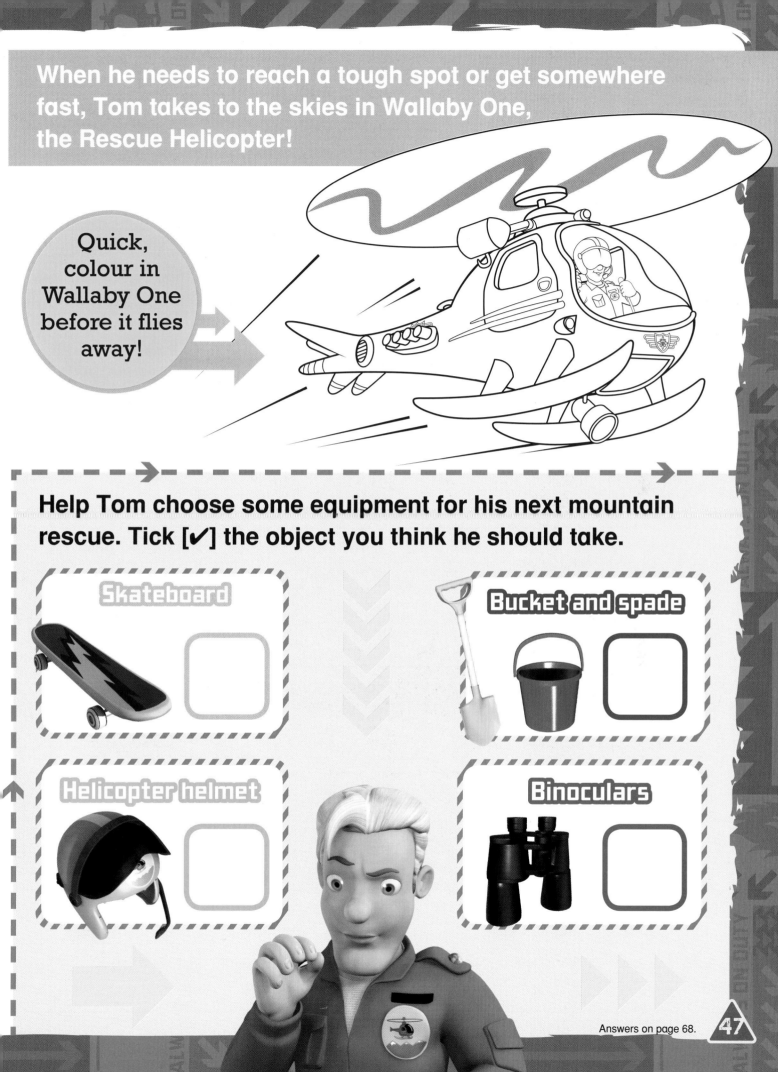

Help Tom choose some equipment for his next mountain rescue. Tick [✔] the object you think he should take.

Skateboard

Bucket and spade

Helicopter helmet

Binoculars

Answers on page 68.

47

COUNTING KIT

Fireman Sam is checking the Fire Station rescue kit. Can you help him? Count how many you can see of each object and write the numbers in the boxes below.

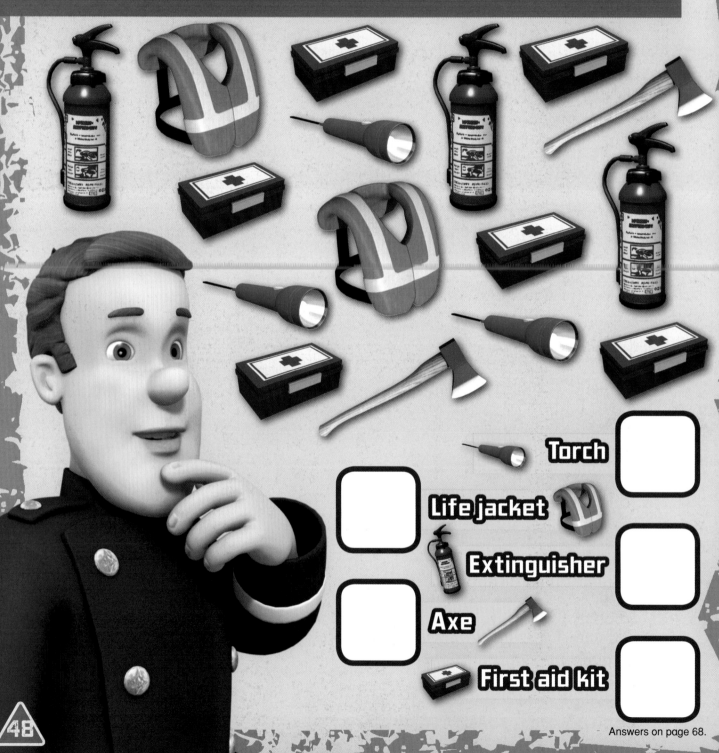

Torch

Life jacket

Extinguisher

Axe

First aid kit

Answers on page 68.

CRAZY CAMERA

Trevor is taking a team photo. But all is not as it should be! Can you spot the 5 things that have gone wrong in his picture?

Answers on page 68.

TREVOR'S TRIP

 *You can help read this story. Join in when you see a picture.*

Trevor   **Dilys**   **Station Officer Steele**   **Norman**

 is taking everyone on a day trip to the

seaside.  has made a picnic to eat on the

beach. Everyone gets on the bus ready to go.

 wants to give the directions using his map,

but  has a new sat nav. "This is the modern

way,"  tells  .

 and  keep arguing about who can

give the best directions. Meanwhile,  is

hungry. When  isn't looking,  helps

himself to a cake from the picnic basket. Soon

 takes another cake!  drives the

bus down a steep, bumpy lane. The bus shakes

and everyone shouts out, especially  !

The bus comes to a halt on some muddy sand.

"This can't be right," worries . The bus is

stuck. Suddenly the tide comes in and the bus is

surrounded by water!  takes charge.

He calls the Fire Station using 's mobile

phone. "Don't worry,"  tells everyone.

"Fireman Sam is on his way."

Fireman Sam gets

everyone to safety

on dry land.

"You can't trust modern gizmos," says  .

"Well, I did need a mobile phone to get help,"

admits  .  opens the picnic basket

to give everyone a nice cake, but the basket is

empty! Everyone looks at  .

 groans and holds his tummy.

Fireman Sam passes him a bucket.

SAM'S SKITTLES

You can play this game on your own or in pairs.

Here's a fun game to play! Make your own skittles by cutting out the pictures of the Pontypandy gang and glueing them onto small plastic bottles.

Collect six small empty plastic bottles to be your skittles.

If you don't have a ball, you could use scrunched-up pieces of paper.

54

Carefully add up the numbers on each skittle you knock down to find out your score!

Wowee! I've scored 8 points!

QUICK QUIZ

James is trying to do this quick quiz. Can you help him? Circle the right answer. Good luck!

Quiz Questions

Station Officer Steele has a beard.	True	False
Dilys runs Pontypandy's shop.	True	False
James and Sarah are twins.	True	False
Penny leads mountain rescue missions.	True	False
Wallaby One is a fire engine.	True	False
Elvis once broke his leg.	True	False
Tom Thomas drives Neptune, the lifeboat.	True	False

Answers on page 68.

DILYS' BIG DAY

It's a big day for Dilys – it's her birthday!

Aw! Thank you, Bronwyn.

Bronwyn gives Dilys a birthday present.

Norman overhears. He'd forgotten it was Dilys' birthday. He hasn't got her a present!

Mam's birthday?! Oh, no!

I'll borrow Mum's gazebo.

I'll bake a cake.

Norman tells his friends. "You could have a surprise party," says Sarah.

The friends all promise to help Norman plan the party.

James goes to the shop to keep Dilys busy, so she doesn't find out about her surprise party.

Can I do anything to help?

Um, OK. You can polish the cucumbers.

Meanwhile, Mandy makes a cake.

Naughty Norman thinks he knows best and keeps adding more flour.

Mandy gets cross and leaves Norman to make the cake on his own.

Mike puts the cake in the oven for Norman.

But Norman fiddles with the timer – he thinks it needs longer to bake.

Um, two hours should do it.

Norman goes to see how Sarah is getting on with the gazebo.

Norman wrestles a pole out of Sarah's hands. He thinks he can put the gazebo up quicker than Sarah.

Sarah walks away in a huff.

When she is gone the gazebo falls down!

Meanwhile, Norman's cake has started to burn. It sets the Floods' cooker on fire!

Mike notices the smoke. He calls Fireman Sam.

Ooooh, Norman!

Sam and Elvis rush to the Floods' house.

They put on their breathing apparatus and enter the kitchen.

As it's an electrical fire, they cut the power first. Then they put out the flames.

Norman rushes up just as Elvis carries out the burnt cake.

"Aw!" sniffs Norman. "I wanted it to be perfect, but it's all gone wrong. I was rotten to Mandy and Sarah and now the cake is ruined."

"Don't worry," Fireman Sam tells him. "We'll help you."

Elvis helps Norman to bake a new cake.

That's right.

Charlie helps the children to put up the gazebo. Bronwyn brings a box of party decorations.

Is it my Norman? What's he up to?

Meanwhile, Dilys is getting suspicious …

Dilys heads out to find Norman and walks straight into her surprise party!

"Did you organise this for me?" Dilys asks Norman.

"Well, I had a little help," admits Norman, sheepishly.

Happy birthday, Mam.

Ah, my little treasure!

PARTYTIME!
FIREMAN SAM SAYS

One person is chosen to be Fireman Sam. They give instructions beginning with "Fireman Sam says …". The other players must mime the action. However, if the instruction does not begin with "Fireman Sam says …" the other players must stay still.

Fireman Sam says … Pat your head to put on your helmet.

Fireman Sam says … Pull on your big fireman's boots.

Swing your arms to take off like Wallaby One!

Fireman Sam says … Sound the siren, Nee-Nah Nee-Nah!

Twitch your nose, like Radar the sniffer dog.

Fireman Sam says … Climb the ladder.

PARTYTIME!
PASS THE BUCKET

You will need two buckets and two teams. Both teams stand in a line.

1. The person at the front of the line holds a bucket. They run round to the back of the line.

2. The team then passes the bucket from person to person, along to the front of the line.

3. The person who is at the front and holding the bucket runs round to the back. Then repeat!

The teams race. The first team to have their first player back at the front of the line wins!

RACE AROUND PONTYPANDY

The Rescue Team are rushing back to the Fire Station. See who can get there first!

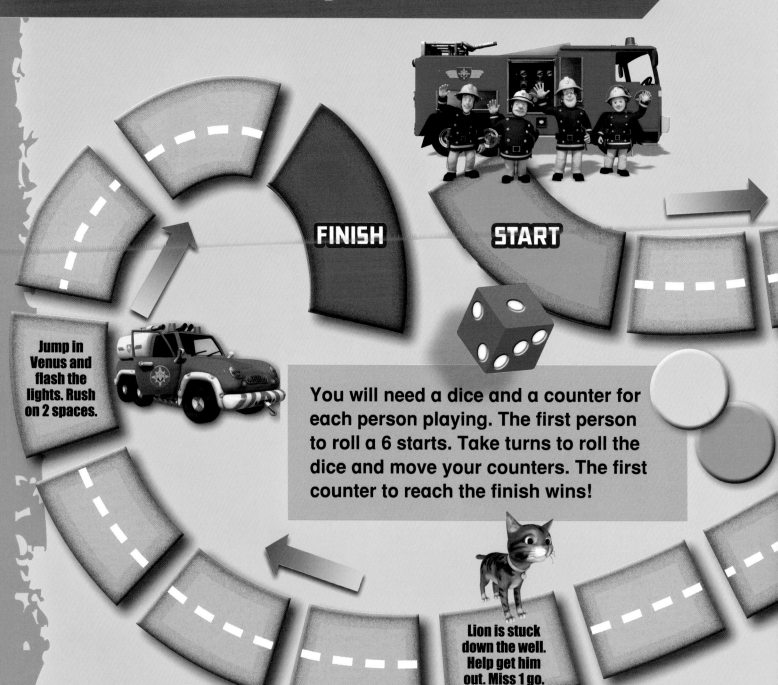

FINISH

START

Jump in Venus and flash the lights. Rush on 2 spaces.

You will need a dice and a counter for each person playing. The first person to roll a 6 starts. Take turns to roll the dice and move your counters. The first counter to reach the finish wins!

Lion is stuck down the well. Help get him out. Miss 1 go.

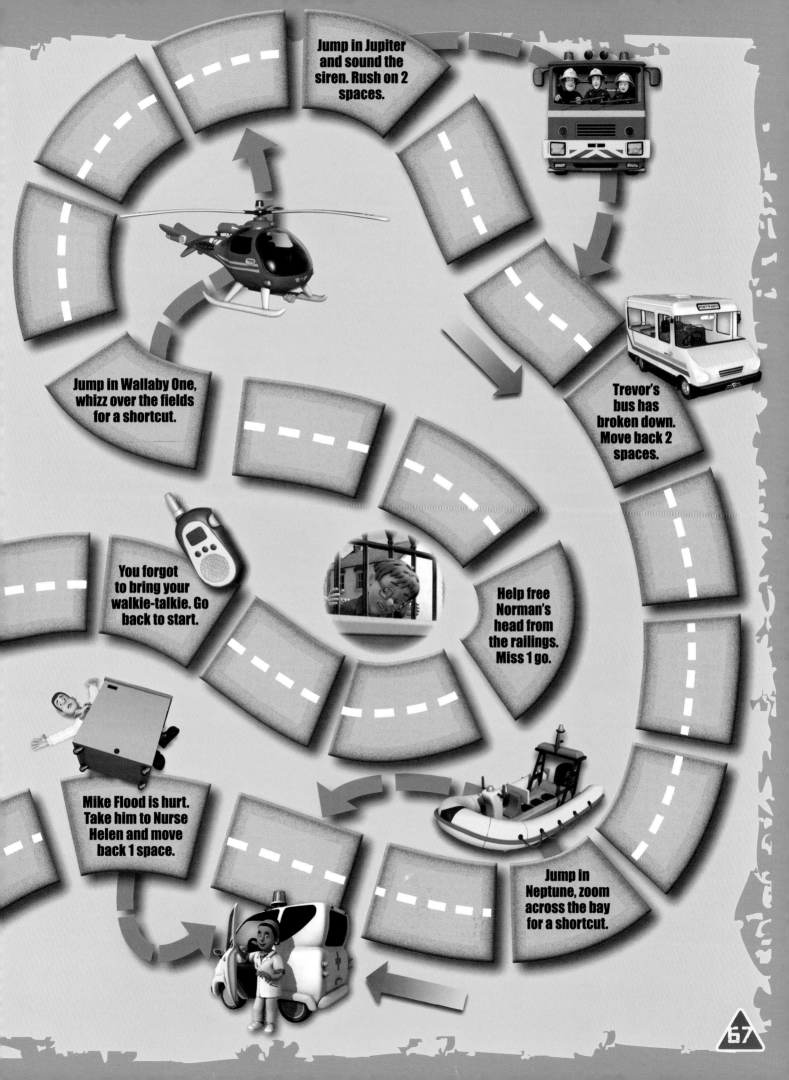

Jump in Jupiter and sound the siren. Rush on 2 spaces.

Trevor's bus has broken down. Move back 2 spaces.

Jump in Wallaby One, whizz over the fields for a shortcut.

You forgot to bring your walkie-talkie. Go back to start.

Help free Norman's head from the railings. Miss 1 go.

Mike Flood is hurt. Take him to Nurse Helen and move back 1 space.

Jump in Neptune, zoom across the bay for a shortcut.

ANSWERS

Fireman Sam and Jupiter put out 7 fires.

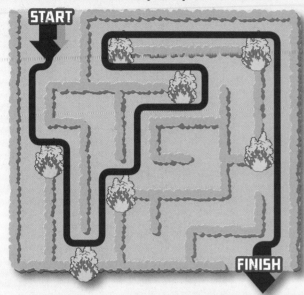

Bronwyn calls Station Officer Steele. Station Officer Steele sends Fireman Sam to rescue Lion. Elvis helps Sam.

Neptune passes 6 whales.

Sam helps Trevor. Elvis helps Norman.

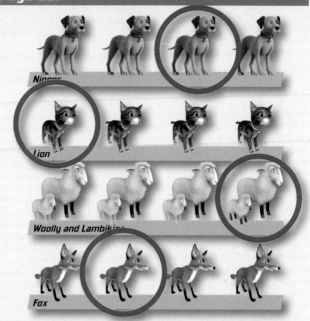

Pictures I and 7 are exactly the same.

Tom should take the helmet and binoculars.

There are 3 torches, 2 life jackets, 3 extinguishers, 2 axes and 6 first aid kits.

False, True, True, False, False, True, False.

I - Penny
2 - Tom
3 - Radar
4 - Norman